Published by Scholastic Inc.
90 Old Sherman Turnpike, Danbury, Connecticut 06816.

ISBN 0-7172-6814-4

Designed and produced by Bill SMITH STUDIO.

Printed in the U.S.A.
First printing, February 2004

In a Jam

A Story About Sincerity

by **Jacqueline A. Ball**
illustrated by
Peter Emslie
and **Teresa Lester**

SCHOLASTIC INC.

New York Toronto London Auckland Sydney
Mexico City New Delhi Hong Kong Buenos Aires

"Mmm," sighed Cinderella, breathing in the sweet smell of roses. "I'm so lucky that picking flowers is part of a princess's duties."

Cinderella had married the Prince and moved into his castle. She had certain royal responsibilities each day.

“Where do we go next, Daphne?” Cinderella asked her lady-in-waiting.

Daphne looked at her list. “The dining room, Princess.”

Daphne crossed off tasks as Cinderella did them.

"You must check the royal teapots . . .

. . . examine the royal goblets . .

. . . select the royal table linens . . .

. . . and inspect the royal serving trays."

"Done!" exclaimed Cinderella.

"Now to the kitchen for the royal tastings," Daphne instructed.

Cinderella had to taste every new recipe prepared by the royal cook and his helpers. The ones she liked were added to the palace menu.

Beatrice, Cinderella's other lady-in-waiting, and Prudence, the housekeeper, stood waiting with the kitchen workers.

Cinderella greeted everyone, and then she tasted a spoonful of lemon custard. "Excellent," Cinderella said.

She bit into a honey-nut muffin. “Delectable!”

Next she nibbled a cucumber-and-watercress sandwich. “Crunchy!”

Cinderella was honest but kind as she offered her opinions.

Then she sipped some cream of pumpkin soup. "Tasty, but it might be even tastier with less salt."

"Yes, Princess Cinderella," the cook answered, making a note.

Afterwards, Daphne helped the cook put things away, and Beatrice and Prudence moved on to their other duties.

Meanwhile, Cinderella greeted the new assistant cook. "Welcome," she said.

"Thank you," he said. "My name is Peter."

Then he held out a plate. On it was a piece of toast covered with glistening green jam. "The pickleberry crop is ripe," he said. "Because I love pickleberries, I made some jam just for you. I hope you like it."

"Oh, dear, I *don't* love pickleberries," Cinderella thought. "But I don't want to discourage Peter on his first day, either."

She took a bite. The jam tasted strong—almost bitter.

"Maybe I don't like it because I don't like pickleberries in the first place," she thought. "Other people may find it delicious."

Peter looked at her anxiously. "What do you think, Princess Cinderella?"

"Princess Cinderella, the seamstress is ready for your fitting," Beatrice announced.

Cinderella smiled. "The taste is very unusual. Thank you for your hard work, Peter," she said as she left for her fitting.

Daphne had noticed Cinderella sampling Peter's jam so she asked Peter for a small bite.

Peter happily spread some on bread for her.

Daphne chewed and swallowed. "It's—quite tasty," she said.

Beatrice entered just in time to hear Daphne's remark. "What's tasty?" she asked.

"This pickleberry jam that I made for the princess," answered Peter eagerly. "Try some."

Beatrice nibbled. "Uh . . . it's scrumptious," she saic

Then Prudence heard Beatrice's remarks and she sampled the jam, too. "Delicious," she said, as she hurried off to do another chore.

Peter was so excited by his success that he raced all over the palace and grounds, handing out slices of bread and jam.

The next morning, Cinderella found a big blob of pickleberry jam on her oatmeal. Carefully, she scraped it off.

But lunch was cheese and pickleberry jam sandwiches. "Why is the jam appearing at every meal?" Cinderella wondered. She hadn't thought it was that good.

"I'll try it again," she decided, "to be sure." Unfortunately, the taste was as bitter as before.

Then Daphne and Beatrice came in, carrying a beautiful new gown.

"Wonderful jam, isn't it?" Daphne asked.

"Well, I'm not that fond of pickleberries," Cinderella replied honestly. "But everyone else must love the jam. It's part of every meal."

Daphne was surprised. "But, Princess, you seemed to like it! That's why I told Peter I liked it, even though I really didn't. I only like strawberry."

"And I was only going along with everyone else," Beatrice said. "I prefer blueberry."

Then Prudence walked in and said she didn't care for Peter's jam, either. "I like orange marmalade best," Prudence told Cinderella. "Actually, nobody in the palace really likes the jam, but no one wanted to say so."

Cinderella looked outside. Workers were carrying baskets of pickleberries into the palace.

"We've caused a big problem," she thought. "We've let Peter think we all liked his jam instead of sharing our true, sincere opinions. Now the situation is getting out of control."

What would a princess do?

Cinderella went to the kitchen and found the cook's entire staff busy making pickleberry jam. Her nose wrinkled at the smell.

"Princess Cinderella!" Peter exclaimed. "Would you like a snack?"

"No, thank you," she answered gently. "Peter, I should have told you I wasn't fond of pickleberries. In fact, I don't think anyone else really likes them."

Peter was confused. "But everyone said they liked the jam," he said quietly.

Cinderella touched his arm. "Often people say things they don't mean because they're afraid of hurting someone's feelings, or because they don't want to disagree. But we all like different things. We should say what we truly feel, as long as we always speak kindly. That is being sincere."

"You like to make jam, and you're very good at it," she continued. "So I have an idea."

He nodded as she explained what she had in mind. Slowly, Peter's smile returned. "I'll get right to work!"

The next morning, the kitchen table held bowls of blueberry and strawberry jam and orange marmalade—as well as *one* bowl of pickleberry jam. The head cook heaped it on his toast.

"You don't have to pretend to like it any more," Prudence whispered to him.

"I'm not pretending," he replied. "I love pickleberries. And I love this delicious jam!"

Peter just beamed, while the others munched happily on the jam each one liked best.

The End